In at the Deep End

With illustrations by
Peter Cottrill

Michelle Magorian

For Jill Bubb

First published in 2016 in Great Britain by
Barrington Stoke Ltd
18 Walker Street, Edinburgh, EH3 7LP

www.barringtonstoke.co.uk

This story first appeared in a different form in *In Deep Water*
(Viking, 1992)

A CIP catalogue record for this book is available
from the British Library upon request

ISBN: 978-1-78112-502-1

Printed in China by Leo

Contents

Chapter 1
The Pool

Ben felt nervous as he stepped out of the men's changing room and headed for the big pool. As he walked, he tried to shake the tension out of his arms.

Most of the lanes were roped off, and at the far end, men and women with clipboards sat under a big banner. They all wore the same red Swimathon T-shirts as the pool lifeguards.

Ben took a deep breath and walked along the side of the pool, past the white plastic chairs and up to one of the men.

"Are you the lap counter for the 12 to 14 group?" Ben asked.

The man smiled up at him. "I am. And you are?"

"Ben. Ben Stevens."

The man ticked Ben's name off the list on his clipboard. "So, where's the rest of your team?" he asked.

"They're coming later," Ben told him. "I'm swimming the first 100 lengths and they're sharing the next 100 between them."

"OK," the man said and he waved at the pool. "You're in lane 4. That's the second one from the far side. If you'd like to wait over there."

'No sweat,' Ben thought, and he strolled over to one of the chairs. He sat down and draped his towel round his shoulders.

Not that he needed it to keep warm. It was boiling and the air was hot and humid. Ben twisted the red swimming cap he'd been given between his fingers and gazed past the rows of flags hanging above the pool to where the clock hung on the wall. Nearly two. He dropped his shoulders and blew out a few breaths. 'Relax,' he told himself. 'No sweat.'

Just then, pop music began to blare out of speakers at either end of the pool. Ben whirled round and shaded his eyes with his hands. The lights seemed brighter than usual, and there were more of them. Balloons surrounded the baby pool. It was now boarded over, and people were sitting at white tables and chairs on the boards, drinking tea and eating biscuits.

To Ben's surprise his stomach was already fluttering. He mustn't get too nervous. Nerves could wear him out.

To pass the time, Ben decided to size up the teams on either side of his lane. He looked at them as if he was looking with Jack and Harry's eyes, and he couldn't help but smile.

On one side were four young men aged between 16 and 18 years old. A stocky man in his 40s was giving them a pep talk. He was waving a stopwatch around as he tried to rev them up. From the man's peaked cap, Ben guessed they were from a youth club. Boy Scout stuff.

Ben, Jack and Harry didn't need to join a club. They just got on and did things. No sweat. Ben felt very proud just knowing that he was at least four years younger than the youth club lot.

'Just look at them,' he thought, 'hanging on the coach's every word, as if this was an Olympic relay final.'

The young men began to shake their legs and stretch out their arms to warm up.

'Daft that they're all here at the same time,' Ben thought. The ones that were swimming the 3rd and 4th legs would be worn out from watching the others by the time their turn came.

At first Ben couldn't see anyone from the team on the other side of his lane. But when he did, his jaw dropped.

The first member of their team was an old woman with curly grey hair. A wrinkly!

Ben turned away and tried not to smile. He was going to be swimming next to a team of wrinklies! He could hear Jack and Harry shriek with laughter and imagine them crashing their powerful elbows into his ribs.

Ben struggled to control himself. He mustn't start rolling around in hysterics. He'd never finish swimming even one length if he did.

Out of the corner of his eye, Ben watched her take off a heavy white robe and pull on her Swimathon cap. It was embarrassing to see someone so old in a black swimsuit.

Chapter 2
A Steady Pace

A voice rang out. "Attention please, everyone!"

Ben sat up straight.

This was it.

A tall man with the strong shoulders of a serious swimmer was talking to them. Ben knew the rules. He didn't have to listen to them. He, Jack and Harry had studied them enough in the sports centre café. No sweat.

But, to his alarm, Ben saw the man approach him.

"On your own?" the man asked.

"The rest of my team are coming later," Ben said.

"He's doing a 100," said Ben's lap counter.

"How old are you?" the man asked.

"I'm 12," Ben said, and added "nearly" in his head. "The others are 14."

The man smiled. "Good on you."

Ben shrugged off the man's remark, but to his annoyance he still felt a flush of pride.

"I need to explain to the other teams that the group at the end will be fast," the man said.

"Don't let that bother you. Take it steady and go at your own pace." And then he smiled. "But since you'll be swimming 100 lengths you're probably aware of that already."

Ben nodded.

"Hello, Betty," the man said, and he beamed at the old woman next to Ben. "Back again?"

So, the wrinkly's name was Betty. Ben shut his ears to their chatter and looked up at the clock.

He would swim a length a minute for about 30 lengths and then begin to slow down.

Two hours he reckoned. Two hours of swimming. Not the best way to think about it. He must pace himself, take it length by length. He could keep adding up how much money each one of those lengths would raise for the children's hospital.

"Everyone ready?" the woman in charge called out.

The coach on Ben's left rested his hand on the back of the first member of the youth club team. "You can do it," he was saying, in a firm voice.

"Big baby," Ben muttered. The teenager was going to be swimming half the distance Ben was going to swim. Ben pulled on his cap and flung his towel to one side.

Betty was already lowering herself into the water. The rest of her team of wrinklies would probably hobble in hours later. That is, if they didn't lose their walking sticks on the way.

Ben was grinning again. 'Focus,' he told himself.

He stood up and slipped into the water.

After only one length Ben was ready to
get out. He couldn't believe how tired he felt.
Perhaps breast-stroke was the wrong one to
choose. But it was his best stroke, the one he
found easiest. He'd never be able to swim front
crawl for 100 lengths.

The swimmer from the youth club in the next lane was having no problems. He was powering up and down in a crawl. A high wave from him sent a gallon of chlorine down Ben's throat and into his eyes. He choked and gasped for breath.

This was a disaster.

'Relax,' he told himself. 'Steady slow pace.'

By the 3rd length he'd got his wind back, but he still felt wiped out. He had steered to the side of the lane, away from the Olympic youth club swimmer, whose high-speed crawl was making waves all round him. Thank goodness the wrinkly was a slower swimmer.

It wasn't until he was ten lengths in that Ben's tiredness lifted. With relief, he realised that it was just that his body had been warming up in the water. That and shaking off his nerves. By length 11, he had worked out a steady rhythm. One that he felt would carry him to 100.

Now Ben started to enjoy himself. He was gliding. There was nothing to think about, nothing to worry about. There was just him and the water, the bright lights, the pumping music, the loud splashing and the voices of the spectators bouncing off the walls. The deafening noise blocked out the world beyond the swimming pool walls.

The first 40 lengths were a doddle. But on Ben's 42nd length, the coach in the next lane started to yell at the teenager in the water. "You can do it! You can do it!"

The three other boys were yelling too, fit to shatter the lights above them.

'Shut up!' Ben thought. He was irritated by the big deal they were making of it.

Ben couldn't see the young man's head, just a flurry of water as he drew closer to the end of the lane. The coach pressed his stopwatch and the next member of their team lowered himself in. Within seconds, the coach had a towel around the first one and was sending someone off to get him a hot chocolate. He was making such a fuss you'd think the boy had climbed Mount Everest or landed on the moon.

Ben turned and pushed off from the wall. As he did so, he twisted round to look for Jack and Harry. No sign of them yet. Still, there was plenty of time.

Chapter 3
The Pressure Builds

"You're nearly there!"

"Atta boy, Calum!"

"It's your best yet!"

"Keep at it!"

And now the penny dropped. The team next to Ben weren't bothered about the number of lengths they swam. They were more worked up about the speed they were swimming. They were after some sort of prize for fastest team. That's what all the fuss was about.

As Ben touched the side of the pool, his lap counter looked up from his clipboard. "You have 12 lengths to go," he said.

And still there was no sign of Jack or Harry. If they didn't arrive soon, Ben's 100 lengths wouldn't count. His team would be disqualified and three months of working himself up to those 100 lengths would be wasted. He wouldn't be able to collect his sponsorship money and his efforts at raising money for the hospital would be scuppered.

As Ben turned at the end of the pool, someone changed the music. The sound rocketed out of the two speakers with such a blast that it nearly spun him over in the water.

As Ben headed back towards his lap counter, he realised that part of what had driven him to do his 100 lengths was the desire to impress Jack and Harry. His two friends towered above him and were built like tanks, so it was important that they knew he was as tough as them. They had to be there to see him swim those 100 lengths. Be there to tell him how amazed they were and slap him on the back even if it stung like a burn when they did.

Then Ben would be one of them. They would be a trio, not a duo and a hanger-on. And he would never feel lost for words with them again, nor would his jokes cause them to gaze down at him with blank faces.

Chapter 4
Teamwork

'Two more to go,' Ben told himself, as he clocked his 98th length.

He felt a sharp stab of jealousy against the team in the next lane. Not for their swimming ability – Ben felt he was just as good – but because they had their mates rooting for every length they swam.

No one was paying the slightest bit of attention to him, apart from his lap counter.

And then he remembered the wrinkly. She was still swimming too, steady and quiet. Ben had been so wrapped up in himself that he hadn't noticed that her team hadn't shown up either.

Chapter 5
The Full 200

Ben swam slowly towards the end of the lane. His heart sank as his fingers touched the wall.

"100," the lap counter said.

Ben rested his arms over the top of the pool.

"What are you going to do?" the counter asked.

Ben had a lump in his throat the size of a fist. 'Do?' he thought. 'Do? Cry my eyes out, that's what I feel like doing.'

"Your team aren't here," the man went on. "Sorry, but that means your 100 lengths don't count."

Ben lowered his head. He didn't dare say anything in case he burst into tears.

Next to him, the youth club crowd were whistling and cheering. If only they'd shut up and the music wasn't so loud, he could think more clearly.

A kind-sounding voice pierced through his misery.

It was the wrinkly.

"What's up?" she asked.

'None of your business, you old prune,' Ben hissed in his head.

"His team hasn't turned up," the lap counter said.

"Can't he keep swimming until they do?" she asked.

"He's already swum 100 lengths."

"I know." The wrinkly turned to Ben. "I've been keeping an eye on you. You've done so

well, even after that shaky start. Come on, keep
going. You can give me some moral support "

'Why should I?' Ben wanted to say. It was
at that moment that he remembered he hadn't
seen any other wrinklies. "Wait a minute," he
said. "Where's your team?"

She pointed to herself. "I'm my team." And
she beamed. "I'm going for the full 200."

"200?" Ben gasped. "But that's three miles!"
And he stared at her, stunned.

"And a bit," she said. "Five kilometres to be
exact."

"Oh, OK," Ben said. "Sorry," he added as he
realised he was staring at her with his mouth
open. But he couldn't help himself. An old
woman like her going for 200 lengths!

She laughed. "Come on, sunshine. Why not
give it a shot?"

Ben looked at his lap counter. "Can I?"

"Sure, if you think you can manage it."

"They'll be here soon, I know they will,"
Ben said. "They've never let me down before.
Perhaps they've been held up somewhere."

The lap counter nodded.

"Let's go," the wrinkly said. She was still
smiling at him.

And Ben found himself smiling back.

Chapter 6
The Deep End

Ben and Betty pushed themselves on.

Ben realised that he really would need to pace himself now.

He relaxed his shoulders again and struck out more firmly with his legs from his hips.

'No,' he thought, 'my mates have never let me down before. But then again I've never asked them to do anything before.'

But he hadn't asked them this time either. They'd volunteered. "No sweat," they had said. "We can swim 50 lengths. Dead easy."

So what had happened to them? Ben pictured them lying in a pool of blood on the High Street. Perhaps they had gasped out some garbled words to the paramedics to tell Ben they couldn't make it, but both had passed out before their vital message could be understood.

Ben touched the wall and turned.

"101 lengths," he murmured.

'Take it easy,' he told himself. 'They'll be here. Maybe there's been another strike on the Tube.'

Jack and Harry were always having trouble with trains. They could be stuck somewhere with no reception, so they couldn't ring the sports centre. Yes, that was it. They'd be in a right stew, cursing and pacing and punching walls.

102 lengths.

Ben blew out into the water. They could be ill of course. Both of them? No. Unless it was food poisoning from a take-away kebab. They were probably puking up somewhere, unable to keep down a drop of water, all strength gone. But then they'd struggle to the door, pick up their towels, still determined to swim those lengths with Ben.

103 lengths.

Chapter 7
A Proper Swimmer

When Ben completed his 150th length, he knew
that Jack and Harry weren't going to make it.

He turned over onto his back to relieve
the stabbing pain in his neck. He had swum
150 useless lengths. Useless, because there was
no way he could swim any further. If he could
get out and have a break then he might make it
to 200, but that would be against the rules and
he would be disqualified.

By now he was past caring. He was so tired he could hardly breathe. He'd take a rest by doing a length or two of slow backstroke before he climbed out.

Betty was still going. He had to call her Betty now. "Wrinkly" was the word Jack and

Harry used for anyone who looked even a tiny bit old, and Ben realised that it didn't suit her at all.

He peered over his shoulder at her. She was a good, strong swimmer with more guts, stamina and staying power than Jack and Harry rolled together. He pictured them making their comments in their tight jeans and fancy trainers, posing and pretending they were macho men.

"Hey, Ben, we forgot," he could hear them saying. "No hard feelings, eh?" Slam of hand on shoulder. "You know how it is?"

'Yeah,' Ben thought. 'I know how it is.'

"Next year, eh?" they'd both say. "Yeah, next year, or the year after."

Ben smiled, but it was a bitter smile. His so-called mates had never intended to come at all. Oh yeah, we can do this. Oh yeah, we can do that. No sweat.

And that summed them up. No sweat. They couldn't produce even a drop of sweat because they didn't do anything. They were all talk.

Yet Ben had longed to be one of them. He had hated feeling tongue-tied and puny and boring. But it wasn't him that was boring. He had just been bored hanging out with the two of them. Bored, bored, bored.

"151 lengths," he muttered.

Why hadn't he seen them for what they were before now? How come he had believed all that bragging and big man stuff?

As Ben floated on his back, a new emotion swept through him. Anger. Anger at Jack and Harry. And anger at himself.

As soon as he touched the wall he turned over and began to swim front crawl. He knew he wouldn't make the 200, but at least if he moved his neck from side to side, it would ease the pain. He lashed out into the water like a tiger released from a cage.

Chapter 8
Hanging On

As Ben crawled length after length, he swam out all the feelings that he had kept bottled up inside him for months. All the doubts he'd ignored when Jack or Harry never turned up for a training session, but told him they were training on other days. How could he have been so stupid?

Because he was desperate to have friends. Any friends. No matter who they were.

When Ben reached 170 lengths the team beside him had finished and they were over the moon, laughing and patting one another on the back.

Betty was still swimming. As if she sensed Ben looking at her, she turned and winked at him.

"Think I'll make it?" she called out.

"Yeah, course you will." He nearly added,
"No sweat," but stopped himself in time.

His neck had eased up now. But the muscles
in his arms felt heavy with tiredness and
his ankles hurt too. He rolled over into the
backstroke again to give himself another rest.

Chapter 9
Victory in Sight

By the time Ben had completed his 180th length, there was no one left in the pool except him and Betty. The only other people around the pool were their two lap counters and a lifeguard perched on a high seat at the side.

The woman in charge came out of the office and looked in Ben's direction.

'Don't let her disqualify me now,' Ben thought.

But the woman raised two thumbs. She was rooting for him! She did the same for Betty.

And then Ben noticed a big smile on the lifeguard's face. Ben hadn't even bothered to look at him before. The lifeguard also gave Ben and Betty the thumbs-up. That was three people who wanted them to make it. It pushed Ben to get the next length done.

Four lengths later, a few more of the centre's staff came out of the office, keen to watch Betty and Ben as they swam on. They seemed relaxed and chilled, not at all bothered at having to stay behind.

The early evening sun had found its way to a long window at the side and its soft light streamed into the pool. Someone had turned the music off. Now it was so quiet that Ben could hear the water lapping around him. In the calm and the sunshine, it felt as though he was swimming in a private pool in Malibu.

Two attendants were removing the flags above their heads.

"Take your time," his lap counter said, when he saw Ben look up at the flags. "Keep to your own steady pace, we're in no hurry."

Ten lengths to go and he knew.

He knew he was going to make it.

'Please don't let me pass out, get cramp or die,' he told himself.

A little group of pool staff was now gathered round his lap counter, who was fighting down a smile.

"Come on, you're nearly there," a tall girl with spiky black hair shouted.

Ben nearly choked. It was the girl that Jack and Harry had fancied for weeks. They'd never even said hello to her, of course. They just

stared at her and talked about her. And here she was, rooting for Ben, not quite 12 years old and puny.

'Correction,' he told himself. 'Puny people don't swim 192 lengths. Three miles. And a bit – nearly.'

Ben laughed. He had no friends and he was laughing in an empty swimming pool. Crazy. But he decided he'd rather be himself and have no friends than try and pretend to be someone he wasn't. And that decision made him feel as light as a feather.

Chapter 10
No Sweat

It was the last length and it was so sweet he didn't want to rush it. Betty knew and she cheered him on from her lane. And then everyone around the pool was clapping. And the woman in charge was clasping her hands above her head.

Ben came in on a slow front crawl, touched the side and hung there, buzzing. He swam to the steps at the side but he felt too weak to pull

himself out of the pool. Pairs of hands grasped
him from above and lifted him up. He had just
reached the chairs when his legs buckled. He
sat down and wrapped the towel round his sore

shoulders. His legs were shaking. His ankles hurt and his feet felt as if someone had stuck them in a fridge. The buzzing was fading fast and all he wanted to do was to collapse into bed and sleep.

"200 lengths," his lap counter said, smiling.

Ben nodded, trying to catch his breath.

The woman in charge caught his eye. "Looks like you didn't need your team-mates after all," she said.

"You're right," Ben said, and he grinned.

She handed him a bottle of water. Ben held it for a moment and then took slow sips. He wanted to sit and take in what he had done.

"200 lengths," he whispered. "I have just swum 200 lengths." He had proved something to himself. He wasn't sure what, but it felt good.

"You'd better get dressed before you get too cold," the lap counter said.

"Not yet," Ben said and he put down his drink.

"It's over now," the lap counter said.

"Not for Betty it isn't," Ben told him.

And he pulled himself to his feet and stumbled over to her lane. Now it was his turn to cheer for her.

Within seconds, everyone else around the pool was joining in. Ben could hardly contain his joy as he watched Betty swim steadily towards the end of her lane.

Once she reached it, she looked up at Ben and clung to the edge, worn out.

"You did it!" Ben yelled down at her. "You did it!"

"A doddle," she gasped, and she waved a trembling hand in the air. "No sweat."

When Ben heard Harry and Jack's two favourite words come out of her mouth, he collapsed with laughter.

"I didn't know I was that funny," Betty said and she smiled. "Do you think I'd make a good stand-up comic?"

"Yes!" Ben blurted out. "No sweat!"

"Hot chocolate all round," the lap counter shouted behind them.

"And helicopter rescue to lift me out of here," Betty added. "My legs have turned to jelly."

But several arms were already guiding her towards the side, where she was helped up the steps.

Within seconds, Betty and Ben had staggered towards one another and were shaking each other's freezing hands.

"Didn't we do well?" Betty said.

But Ben was still laughing too much to reply.

Our books are tested
for children and young people by
children and young people.

Thanks to everyone who consulted on
a manuscript for their time and effort in
helping us to make our books better
for our readers.

More *4u2read* titles ...

Going Batty
JOHN AGARD

As a rule, Shona doesn't hate any living thing, but she really can't stand bats. And that's pretty unfortunate – she not only has a bat project to contend with at school, but there's a bat colony in the attic!

Will Shona go ... batty?

If Only We Had a Helicopter
ROGER McGOUGH

The sky above spun slowly round and round.

"If only we had a helicopter," I said, "we'd find the treasure in a couple of minutes."

"But we haven't," Midge said. "So it's no use thinking about it."

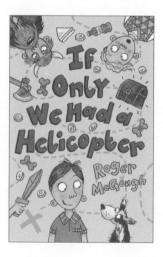

Amber's Song
GILLIAN CROSS

Scream, SCREAM, SCREEEAM!

That's Mark's house since baby Amber arrived. And there's no peace at school either.

Mark's band has a gig coming up, but everyone is in fighting mood. Can Mark find a way to help them all work together on their new song, or will there be red faces all round — not just baby Amber's?

Contact
MALORIE BLACKMAN

Contact is forbidden.

No handshakes. No hugs. Even sport is virtual.

But Cal and his mates are tired of playing by the rules ...

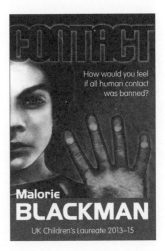

www.barringtonstoke.co.uk